LITTLE
BEAST

JULIE DEMERS
TRANSLATED BY RHONDA MULLINS

Coach House Books, Toronto

Canada Council   Conseil des Arts      Canadä
for the Arts   du Canada

Coach House Books acknowledges the financial support of the Government of
Canada through the National Translation Program for Book Publishing, an initia-
tive of the Roadmap for Canada's Official Languages 2013–2018: Education,
Immigration, Communities, for our translation activities. We are also grateful
for generous assistance for our publishing program from the Canada Council for
the Arts and the Ontario Arts Council. Coach House Books also acknowledges
the support of the Government of Canada through the Canada Book Fund.

*Please note that the publisher is aware that the characters in this novel use vocabulary
and stereotypes appropriate to the setting of the book, 1944 in rural Quebec – namely
the word 'Indian' and a clichéd depiction of Indigenous people. We apologize for any
discomfort this may cause.*

LIBRARY AND ARCHIVES CANADA CATALOGUING IN PUBLICATION

Demers, Julie, 1987-
[Barbe. English]
        Little beast / Julie Demers ; translated by Rhonda Mullins.
Translation of: Barbe.
ISBN 978-1-55245-366-7 (softcover)
        I. Mullins, Rhonda, 1966-, translator II. Title. III. Title: Barbe.
English.
PS8607.E487595B3713 2018   C843'.6   C2018-900935-7
                                                        C2018-900936-6

Little Beast is available as an ebook: ISBN 978 1 77056 553 1 (EPUB), ISBN 1
77056 554 8 (PDF).

To Pierre-Alexandre Fradet,
for his love and inspiration

I

Rivière-à-Pierre, the Gaspé Peninsula, winter 1933. I remember it well because I was already the flicker of an idea in Mother's belly.

That was the year Mother couldn't stand up without help: pregnancy had her by the jugular. The family had turned their backs on her because she and Father had gotten caught up in the ultimate sin. Which is to say, they had touched each other's difference.

So, winter 1933. I had spent the previous few months ruminating in Mother's abdomen. I was bursting with life, which my arms and legs expressed without mercy. To help me settle, Mother would rain down fists on the refuge in her belly.

Being a fetus is serious business. It's not like being an internal parasite; it's a constant effort. There is no respite. Particularly since fetuses are responsible for the person carrying them but can do nothing to help them. As a fetus, I tried to help Mother. I pampered her. I made her laugh.

I distracted her from her dark, unwholesome, smutty thoughts. But I soon figured out that I wasn't quite up to the task. It doesn't pay to get carried away with extreme thoughts. For instance, you can't keep thinking about what it would look like if a fetus murdered an adult, although it is a serious topic that merits consideration.

I would often ponder these questions, and Mother had probably had enough of my philosophical musings. That is no doubt why, a few months before the due date, she lay down on her back and evicted me like a common tapeworm.

If I ever decide to return to the village, maybe she will still want me. Mother needs to be pampered, and I would do my best, just as I did when I was inside her belly.

II

Outside, there is a long trail that I never take that leads to where the people are. In a different way, it also leads to where I am and where the people never go. It is a narrow, hilly trail, filled with dirty depressions and wolf traps. It's impossible to get here wearing leather sandals – it's useless to even try. Getting to me requires boots. Men's boots.

One fine morning, I found my shelter waiting for me here. It had been disfigured by the burrs and the thorns and sat trembling on a pile of rocks. I smoothed out the rough edges and knit it curtains. I showed it some kindness, and now it stands tall. Now, my cabin and I lay our heads down between two mountains, safe, from dusk to dawn.

Soon weeks will have passed that it has sheltered me. Soon weeks will have passed that I have been willing. I have fallen for it, I love it, because I love all that is big and that has as few doors as possible. You can lose yourself inside and never come out.

The forest that surrounds me opens wide onto the rest of the world, treetops pointing to the sky. It is a deep, devout forest. It is meditating; its thoughts are carried on the wind through the leaves, like thousands of prayer flags. It made itself from wood, petals, and needles. When I headed toward it for the first time, the woods grabbed hold of me. The trees formed a phalanx, surrounding me. Frozen, hunched over, I noticed the earth swirling over my tracks, erasing them, and with them the possibility of heading back the way I came.

I closed the doors to my shelter and I don't open them anymore. I let the insects, nuts, and branches drop on the roof. The wind has stopped whistling through the walls, but everything is in danger of collapsing. No matter, I tell myself. Better to be buried than to surrender. This I know from experience: if the outside gets in, the outside will win.

When I was little, everything conspired to beat a path to my door, with the light leading the charge. Now I understand that there is just one way to cope: cut off access to everything. Lock the deadbolt. Stop the light and the sound from getting in. People think music is innocent. They think that melodies, particularly lullabies, are a source of comfort. But don't be fooled: you need to stop everything from finding a crack and making its way in.

These things are learned. Right here, right now, there is nothing. There is no one. Not even a hint of colour. Not even the sliver of an atom of anyone. I have but one head, and I am alone in it. There is nothing left except for blackness. Not the colour black, just blackness.

No doubt at this very moment someone somewhere has their eyes closed. And they aren't thinking about me. When your eyes are closed, there are better things to do than to think about others. I didn't go into quarantine with anyone. No one wants to be quarantined with me. And I don't want to be quarantined with them. Frankly, when you are wise, like me, it's probably best.

III

The animals' howls slip under the door. An entire bestiary is pawing at the cabin walls. But I know the animals won't come in. I'm not scared, no way.

Everything in my safe haven is calm and suspended in mid-air. The steam from the pots coats the walls of the cabin and clings to the windows. The wood is so damp that mould blooms on it. I let the water boil to watch the liquid go where it will – a massive wave receding. All around me the walls close in and calm me. The floor creaks. The dust accumulates. Particles of it fall and fall, and fall some more.

The provisions, left here by someone else and stored in the crawl space under the floor, are dwindling. So far, I've crunched on sixty-seven apples, peeled thirty carrots, sliced twenty-two cabbages, and boiled I don't know how many potatoes. All that is left is a bag of turnips. Thirty-six rancid turnips, to be precise.

My worldly possessions fit in a tanned hide bag: three pencils, a penknife, a sewing needle, two ration stamps, a book of matches, marbles, and a notebook. There is also an old hare lying on the table, no life, no breath.

It takes military discipline to keep track of time. When I wake up, I look through the window to study the traces of things that have passed this way, the signs of time elapsing, trails in the snow that keeps on snowing. I spot hooves and claws. I study the migration of species. Traces of blood don't scare me one bit. As long as there are no boot prints in the snow, I'm in no danger. Once my worries lift and I am certain that the Boots are far away, I add a mark to my 1944 Gaspésie calendar.

I look out at the storm that just keeps storming. There, right out there, the bushes, the animals, and the dens are being buried in snow, the ice bridges are collapsing. All around, animals have built coffins of ice. They stay awake by blinking an eye, as if they have put life in parentheses, and I alone watch winter without joining in, my forehead resting on the window pane. I don't even dare stick my nose outside. If I were to open the window, my nostrils would freeze shut; they would stick together, and it would be the end of me. It is hard to bring the outside in. It always hurts a little.

There is no smoke rising up through the branches around me. There are no human smells (dirty, foul smells).

Only a few animals know the way here. They are called wolves, cougars, flying squirrels, moose, and deer. When we come face to face, we look at each other the way we would look at a foreigner, with a mix of respect and fear. Sometimes guile wins, and it is better to stay hidden. We recognize each other by our tracks.

I take Hare's body and press it to my chest. I take my chest and press it to Hare's body. He spent the night by the fire, and now, even though he is gone, it is like he is here. I rock him and hear him purr. He digs a delicate furrow in my neck. Hare looks at me through beady little eyes set in his eye sockets, and even though he is dead, we still love each other with a love that cannot be denied.

Sometimes I take him with me to the cistern. The water, the heat, and our bodies pressed against each other make us forget that we are not of the same species. What purpose does a species serve, anyway?

I look Hare and his furry, grey pelt up and down. I grab his body, squeeze it, press my face into his carcass. The smell of his decay envelops me. With his big, wild eyes, Hare tells me it is my fault he has no more flesh, that he isn't moving. Yes, I was a formidable trapper. I had loads of snares. I put them in the forest, hoping to collar the necks of the living. Preening animals let themselves be trapped; that is what happened to Hare. It was a long time ago, in the village of Rivière-à-Pierre, before the cabin doors shut forever, never to be opened again, and I lost face.

Rivière-à-Pierre. The name paints an image. I can see my village from here. Yes, I can see it, I swear, with my eyes that remember. The men bring home their bodies and their prey. Their beards are longer than before. The women's cries are as plaintive as can be. Mother wears her shawl of misery over her hunched shoulders.

The memories are vivid.
    But I must fight them.
    But the memories are vivid.
    But I must fight them.

No.
    It's not weakness.
    Yes.
    It's a wave of fatigue.

IV

Before I ended up here, I was somewhere else. I was in a place where there is no forest, no trail, no cabin. I lived on the riverbank filled with trawlers in a village that only the river bothered with. There was a school, a fountain, and a mill. You could run along the rooftops and throw apples at the gulls. The church bells chimed and sometimes the horns trumpeted. At noon, the sun beat down on the face of Christ, and it was like a revelation.

In the village, I was bound by the north and its polar magnetism; its power reached the place where the river lies dying, right there, at the foot of the mountains. Huge branches of the river stretched out as far as the eye could see to bash at the ravines. Its tides ate away at the banks. Worn-out fishing huts piled up against the cliff faces. Teetering, huddled together, they held their breath until they were smashed by the tides, offering up a few rotten wooden planks to the sea.

In the village, the river calls to its death anything that cares to live near it. For centuries, white birds have plummeted into the waves. Sailors and their sea legs follow closely behind, surrendering to the depths like wreckage. Whales – those virtually imperceptible giants of the water – martyr themselves on the beach. They lie dying for a day, two days, three days … too long, at any rate.

Every summer, Christians make the climb to plant a cross on the summit of Mont St. Pierre. Every winter, the gusting winds hurl the cross into the water. In my village, everything done is done in vain.

The dormer window in my grey bedroom looked out over the river's rage. With my nose pressed to the glass, I counted the masts of sea-worn boats bobbing wildly, measured the force of tides, and feared for the drowned. Whether I looked to the east or the west, whether it was winter or summer, I was hemmed in. And not just by the river and the mountains. I roamed only as far as the line Mother drew. My comings and goings stopped at the walls and the locked doors. I was strictly obliged to watch the outdoors from my hiding place behind the curtains. I had to see without being seen.

I never went to school, although school tried to come to me. When the priest, the notary, and other authorities came to the house, they were greeted by Mother's contemptuous silence. They would lecture her, but they always left, their arguments spent. Mother would tell me that I didn't have a head for language or what it took to learn the classics. I expressed myself with my face.

Mother's lessons would start at daybreak. She would heat water on the stove, then fill a basin until its thirst was quenched. The first sunbeams would come in through the sheer curtains on the window, encounter the steam, and die on Mother's face. She would take off her nightgown and let the water run down her chest. Because Mother was naked, I would listen to what she said and mimic her gestures. I wanted to show her that I was a woman despite my face.

Carried by her tongue, Mother's words permeated me. Her familiar voice took over my vocal cords. Her words thrust themselves into my throat and came out blaring. In the worst of my worst moments, Mother's melodies became my language. I must have been made for it – it is my mother tongue, after all.

Sitting at Mother's dressing table, I spent hours looking at myself, trying to make out the sort of woman my features foretold. I imagined myself a lascivious redhead, an innocent blond, a buxom brunette. But at age nine, the mystery gradually lifted. I lost the enigma of youth, my beauty in draft form, my promise of a work in the making. At age nine, I was already complete. The hint of apple that sometimes coloured my cheeks had turned to cider. When I looked at my reflection in the mirror, I no longer imagined the future. I would grab the present by the scruff of the neck, reach for Mother's cosmetics and creams, and hide my face. All women perform a comedy of manners when putting on makeup; I learned to be a clown.

I worked on enduring my reflection. I was on the verge of accepting that having to live with myself was an endless bore and that looking at myself in the mirror would bring me no joy. 'Be satisfied with your looks,' Mother would say. But I would repel everyone. I would end up scaring males: grimy old men and ugly runts alike. They would lock me in my bedroom and shake me, each one harder than the last. Only beautiful things are precious: those who have to be satisfied with their looks can be shaken silly.

My face didn't belong to me. It took over my entire being. It came with me wherever I went. For me, existing involved my face, and facing the world meant showing it. Which is why, as a precautionary measure, Mother closed everything: the doors, the windows, the curtains, even her eyes when she had to look at me.

I was the only one who could read the passage of time on faces. Between when Father left and when he came home, his beard would have grown. Between when Father left and when he came home, I would have grown older. But he didn't see me; when Father came back from the bush, he didn't bother looking at me. He came back only for Mother. He came back to touch her difference.

I was always alone; Mother was the only one who ever came close to me. But her voice whispered too many maudlin things to ring true, truly true. I could see her tremble in my presence. She told me the kinds of things that one says but that don't need repeating. She told me that the world is ugly and not worth the effort. She told me that you shouldn't lift your skirt or walk alone in the forest, because there are dirty old men waiting for just that. She told me that you shouldn't drink or eat too much, you should be desirable but let yourself be desired, be unforgettable but be forgotten, don't let the sunlight in, remember the curtains, if people saw us what do you think they would say? The sun is for outside, happiness is for later, whatever you do don't forget to say your prayers, and don't bite your nails, always listen to Father and when he talks to you bow your head, when he scolds you bow it even more, don't expect anything from life, anyway there is nothing more, climb up on my lap, come into my arms, take this slap, don't duck the blows, and keep smiling.

Every day in the cabin, my pen flits above the cistern. I write for posterity, but also to replace Mother's words with my own. If someone finds me, they can gather my remains and file my thoughts by topic and date. If, on the other hand, scientists eventually manage to bring the dead back to life but hesitate to do so as a matter of right, be they advised: I want them to revive me. I hereby give them permission.

V

Death doesn't scare me. It's not the end – even temporary – that frightens me. Only coming face to face with the Boots puts the fear of God into me. When they come – and I know they will come – I would like to be able to choose my mask. I'd smell like beer, whiskey, and musk. Have short, tousled hair. Know how to piss a good distance and take a long dump, with a newspaper. There is something unfair about not being able to choose your face: it's like heading down a road that you know is going nowhere.

I get ready for the trenches. I prepare my armour and check my equipment. I have hung snares in the windows, curse words on the doors. I have made traps, erected barricades. I practise my battle cry and do drills. With concentration, I crane to look at my whiskers.

I awoke to a gunshot one night, and I haven't slept since. I keep tossing and turning. I know that the Boots are striding this way, sniffing my tracks. They will eventually find my safe haven and make it unsafe.

I feel that the end is nigh, but my body does what it wants. Every time I move, my spine compresses. I pop and I crack. One day, for sure, I will be hollow and worn-out. I will disappear for good through the cracks in the floor. In the meantime, my nails grow and break.

Even though Hare is dead, he is aging. He is losing his fur and doesn't keep me warm like he used to. Soon he will be good for nothing.

Misfortune never strikes but once, and so water is dripping through the cabin's roof. I have to rip up the floorboards to place them over my head. The water stops dripping on my face, but now my feet are numb.

I've run out of wood. Yesterday, I burned the chairs. Soon it will be the sheets. I reach my hand toward the flames. It's like kissing a man: it's hot and dangerous. The air smells of old age, and smoke catches in my throat. I cough, exhausting myself, and cover my nose with my hands. I hold my breath, but I prefer suffocation to the cold outside. I stay in the shelter.

I plunge my head into the water. I open my mouth and swallow. The water shoots up my nose, into my throat and my lungs, and I hear a roar. My limbs go limp, and death tugs at my toes. And then it happens: My head rises from the water.

Lying in the cistern, I see the forest. One window is all that separates me from it. I listen to the waves of cold pound against the walls. They are trying to devour the cabin. To stop it from collapsing under their strength, I jump up and hurl my body against the walls. I stand with my feet as far apart as they will go. I stretch my arms as wide as I can. And the snow falls. And the trees ice over. And the valleys fill up. And the mountains grow older.

And that's okay with me, I think.

VI

'You're not a monster,' Mother used to say. 'Just a little beast.'

For Mother, even though I was becoming a woman, I was still slender, something that can be caressed but that shouldn't be caressed. The more my little face grew, the more Mother turned her breasts away from it. The first weeks, she cried like a baby, but she quickly learned to deal with my distinctive feature. She spent hours touching my chin, my hair, pressing her nose into my beard. In her mother's voice, she would whisper that I must never leave the house. That the people outside wouldn't understand. That, at best, they would understand only later.

So there was nothing to be done but to stay indoors, quiet and watchful. Nothing was supposed to change, and nothing did. I would leave my bedroom at night, only at night, at the same time as the flying fish. I would crawl through the dormer window and, like them, emerge in the light of the moon.

But my adventures and misadventures never went very far. My victims were hardly worthy of the name. While everyone slept, I would sneak into cottages and move things around. Sometimes, just sometimes, driven by the desire for real adventure, I wouldn't put things back where they belonged before dawn. A mackerel would appear on the shoemaker's counter. The seamstress would have to bend down and pick up her rosary. The lumberjacks would have to go to the living room for their gin. Yes, they were serious crimes, but they would be forgotten soon enough.

Mother no longer slept at night. She would stay up reading unreadable books, which she kept under lock and key in a dresser in the living room. One night, I hid in the wardrobe to watch her. She read out loud, and the words told of even more serious crimes than the ones reported on the radio. The next morning, I opened my French notebook and the dictionary for the first time. The day after that, I opened the bible.

I liked the bible. I liked it because it was so thick that it seemed I would never finish it, and since I had been told that people cannot die without having read it cover to cover, I figured that I would never die if I read it slowly, eternally.

Mother had turned away from the bible: she was with-
ering away, slowly but surely, and wouldn't let anyone in
the house anymore. Except for one night, when I must
have been ten years old, when Mother offered hospitality
to a beggar woman. Mother felt sorry for her because of
her face. Mother always felt sorry for faces.

I never saw the beggar woman's face, but you don't
need to see a face to know that it arouses pity. Sometimes
the voice is enough. Mother asked her for news of the
lumberjacks and the war. The old woman told her what
she knew. The rest she made up.

The next day, after she had gone, a trunk appeared in
the middle of the living room. It was filled with books.
Why did she leave them for us? It's a mystery. In any
event, flipping through them, I discovered that I already
knew just about everything: the name of the earth's
animals, the Ten Commandments, the trajectory of
comets, the outcome of elections and battles in the East,
the names of baseball teams. All of it had been explained
to me by the bible, or by Mother, or on the radio. The rest
was already inside me. There was nothing more for me to
learn, or at any rate, very little.

I spent the best years of my life looking through *The
Thermosiphon* and *Balloons and Air Travel*, although I
really enjoyed reading *Apparent Death and Real Death:
Assisting the Dying in Body and Spirit*, the celebrated book

by Dr. Desroches. Between books, I would faithfully watch Mother's daily naps, as she would often sleep in the afternoon. Dr. Desroches was the one who told me that the best way to go unnoticed is to play dead. So Mother was playing dead.

While I slowly gained confidence, Mother persisted in not thinking for herself. We kept the doors and windows shut, but the humans from Rivière-à-Pierre kept overrunning our porch. We were invaded by their voices; they told us how it was going to be. The things I heard through the boards were about me. Things that crouch in the depths but that later resurface. Things that I force myself to forget but that are stronger than forgetting.

It started innocently enough, almost without warning: 'You have to take her out for some fresh air. What are you feeding her? What are you teaching her?' Then it would continue like this: 'Is she an idiot? Do you still breastfeed her? Do you still hold her hand?' And then, at age seven: 'Enough childishness, lies, and foolishness. She isn't an infant anymore. She has to stop acting like a baby. Look in the mirror. Other people don't behave like this.'

I didn't matter that Mother put thicker and thicker curtains on the windows; we could still hear the voices. They got in through the ears and made their way through the skull. Once they got inside the head, they would make it split and crack. The nonsense would slip inside, slip so far inside it almost came back out. But it would stay in there, surviving, lying dormant within us. Nonsense is surprising at first, but after a bit there is nothing surprising about it, and soon it makes every gesture not so innocent. I wash my hands. I scrub my nails. I brighten my complexion. I don't yawn like I used to. I don't sneeze like I used to. I don't talk, I don't laugh, I don't play anymore. Constantly, at every moment, I put my hand in front of my mouth because putting your hand in front of your mouth is supposed to change everything.

And one day the passersby no longer stopped in front of the porch. They looked down at the ground but they still eyed us; they closed their mouths but showed their teeth. I thought we would finally get a bit of peace, but it was not to be because Mother kept opening her mouth. And it kept on. It started over, only more so: Don't get your clothes dirty (particularly on Sunday). Watch you don't stain them (particularly on Sunday). You have to be careful not to show your underwear (even if it's beautiful). You have to be polite and say 'hello' and not 'hi' like a boor, say 'excuse me' and not 'whoops' like a boor. You don't have to suffer to be beautiful but be beautiful to suffer, always write in cursive script (because it looks neater), always smile with your mouth closed (because it looks neater), always lower your eyes in front of men and be charming honest virtuous reserved timid docile. Don't complain if there is violence at lunch. Be fresh and ready for anything and when I say anything, I mean anything.

But fear not, no no no. Our village is the best village in the world, and our world is the best world there is. But just think about that for a minute. We have always lived in a village. So how can we not be favourably disposed to it? How can we not love it from the bottom of our hearts? How can we not cherish it like we cherish a mother? Here's my theory: the love we feel for Rivière-à-Pierre results from an emotional attachment. If you love Rivière-à-Pierre unconditionally, it's because you haven't cut the umbilical cord. I cut the cord posthaste, and now my village makes me sick. It generates deep hostility in me. I think the whole world should agree that the village leaves a bitter taste in the mouth. I will hear no further argument: the village is ugly. A new verifiable fact, an accepted idea, a universal truth. Yes.

VII

The night I left the village, there was no one in the fields and no one on the road and no one on the shore of the river. But I wasn't alone. Mother was staring off into space. With Father gone, Mother's arms were no longer good for anything. She no longer argued, no longer moaned. She was fading without disappearing. She would station herself at the window and talk to her reflection. When her body would flag, she would undo her blouse and beat her chest until her breasts were bruised. I would watch her from a distance turning into a saint, and I would curse God out of jealousy: it was a sign I wasn't cut out to be a martyr.

Unlike Mother, I hadn't kneeled in a long time. I would go up on the roof when they were calling for a storm and stare out at the spray from the river. I would spread my arms wide and welcome the gusts. My lungs would fill with seaweed, and not just the smell; they would literally fill with seaweed. Heeding my call, the waves would gain strength. They would lick the sides of the roads. Eventually, I would turn to catch my breath, and I would see the mountains, standing tall and beautiful. Unyielding: they were unyielding. They laid their weight on my shoulders, immense, my height. Have I mentioned that I am tall?

You have no idea what it is like to be a child. I am no longer one – I'm eleven years old now – but still I remember. In Mother's arms it smelled like warm milk, a housewife's toil, and the fear of infidelity, and it was easy to stay caught in there. It's always different in the arms of another: the smell can surprise you.

They say that kids want to stay little. That they want to stay tiny and fragile, their heads up their butts. People who say this were never little. Truth be told, some children's main ambition is to grow old and wrinkly fast. Some little ones want arthritis as soon as possible. I don't dream of a fountain of youth; I dream of wrinkles, the sooner the better.

But you have to know how to grow old. If you age badly, you cling to others like to Mother's droopy breasts. When you are old and ugly and no one is interested in your difference anymore, you are left to die in peace. And then, finally, you are released.

The night I left the village, the males had had enough of Mother's silence. They came out of nowhere. They invaded the fields, the roads, the shores of the river. Torches in hand and guns slung across their chests, they marched up the pebble path and stormed the family porch. When there was no answer at the door, they broke it down.

'We have a decree,' one of them shouted. 'Tell us where the girl is,' another said. A third man grabbed Mother and pinned her to the floor. She started to cry. She begged them not to go upstairs, to leave me alone. Me, alone, her little beast.

The males headed for the stairs. Their boots made the stairs creak. They were heavy, very heavy, too heavy, even heavier than Father's.

The men came upstairs regardless, and I could hear their breath – the breath of males who are panting. Stopping in front of the door, they put their dirty paws on the door handle. But the door wouldn't open. Locked.

The men broke it down with a battering ram.

They came in. Their smell preceded them: leather, tobacco, and sweat. Then their bodies appeared: tall, with broad shoulders, even broader than Father's.

I was crouching behind a trunk. With my back to the window. The sky was overcast. They didn't see me.

I saw them. The darkness shrouded their faces, but I saw them. I was not imagining things: they really were there. A mountain of beard and muscle. Five men, maybe six. I could barely distinguish their heads from their bodies. Two of them stepped forward. One had Christ hanging around his neck, and the other was a male like a hundred others.

'I'm Mayor Harrison, and this is the parish priest, Father Arsenault.'

I raised my head.

'You're a good little girl. Your mother, Rose-Marie, has told us a lot about you. We want to talk.'

So they wanted to talk.

Their shoulders were tensed, but they just wanted to talk.

All they ever did was talk. They were nothing but voices.

'We want to talk about your future.'

I wasn't listening to what they were saying: Christ was still shining on the cross. I liked that he was shining, but I would have preferred he shine somewhere else: in my hands. I could have stepped closer and gotten a better look at him. Yes, I could have approached without them noticing. The sky was overcast, they wouldn't have seen me. No one other than Mother and Father had ever seen me with this thing. And no one else would ever see me.

There was no danger.

I stood up. I advanced. They held their breath. Their smell got sharper. The mayor had been drinking. The priest smelled like a woman's flesh. I advanced. The mayor's hands were calloused, and the priest's were covered in ink. I advanced. The clouds were gone from the sky. Christ was shining brighter and brighter. I could almost touch him. Reach him. Kiss him.

The moonlight made it like daytime.

I stopped advancing: I saw them. I saw their faces.

And they saw me. Saw my beard.

They stopped talking; they stared at me.

Then Mother screamed. Mother struggled. Mother started up the stairs. Mother climbed. Mother was grabbed from behind. Mother fell. Mother broke away. Mother got back up. Mother kept going. Mother came into the bedroom. Mother saw me. Mother rushed to me. And I yelled, 'Mother, a man is pointing a gun at you.' Mother turned, and the man pointed his gun at me.

The dormer window.

I'd escape through the dormer window.

Mother, goodbye. And goodbye to the village and the fountain and Christ on the cross that tells the time like a revelation. I took the longest road. I followed the pebbles, walked along the river, scrambled up the cliffs. I advanced against the current, with my back to the barking, away from the sound of the Boots. I dodged the bullets, fell in the ditch, ripped my tights. I tripped a hundred times and scraped my knees a hundred times more, but eventually I found it, my shelter.

And yet, nothing's to say they won't find me and put a rope around my neck, the Boots.

VIII

B^{ut} At this moment

    The wind is shaking the cabin.

    The sun is dropping behind the woodland caribou.

    And I have just enough time to say that my face doesn't match my head.

I get out of the tub.

    My words are clean again.

    I stop writing.

And then, no, I continue.

    To be honest, I never stopped writing. I even wrote in the white space. I always write, or almost always. I have to write this story before the Boots find me. I want them to find my words before they find my face.

The storm complicates things. The beams creak, the ceiling groans, the forest competes with the walls of my refuge. The ground and the air become one: everything is turning to dust, smoke, particle. The noises outside turn to rock. Through the creaking of the wooden boards and the silence of the animals, I breathe.

Outside comes in. Droplets of water make their way between the walls. The walls of the cabin pitch, the floor floats. The water is icy. I bend, I curl, I straighten. Not that I'm scared, but it's about to spill over.

I'm cold. I breathe in, I breathe out. I make sure my own heat reaches me. I want to soak up my smell.

Lapse in concentration. The words spill over the margins. So I continue my story on the beams, on the walls. I press my pencil into the soft wood. To visit me is to read me. Or these words will be taken to my grave.

A new sentence. I pull my pencil out of the soft wood and let it slide along the pages. I write as if I'm stuttering, but I feel I have to continue nonetheless. Because no one else can say 'I' in talking about me.

A jolt.

A roar.

My pencil glides_____

No, I won't lift my head; no, I won't turn away from my notebook. Nothing can surprise me anymore, and nothing can make me rush. You can get used to anything, it turns out. An elm fell on the cabin. Its branches came through the roof, but it doesn't matter: I'll get used to it, because you can get used to anything.

Rustling, growling, a ruckus, a snout pops out of the branches. The horror. If I let him, he will make himself comfortable, like the man of the house. He will spread his scent, his fur, his orders, his blows all around. I don't like it. I hate cohabitating. I want a place all my own in the cemetery. I'm alone for a reason. Out, foul beast! I drool, I growl, and worse, I talk. I know how to deal with animals: you have to scare them with words because the only thing they understand is yelling.

I rip up the weakened floorboards. Standing on the tub, I am almost tall enough to touch the roof with my fingertips. I shove the boards in the hollows of the branches. I write on the boards: *goodbye animals, goodbye bad weather.*

The beams collapse.

Damn.

The wind whistles through.
Damn.

The wind goes for my notebook, rips the sheets, and my writing flies away. The pages scatter and fall into the tub. I run, I grab them. I save a few before they founder.

No.
   No.
   I am in a safe place.

I just have to write out loud to make it so.

(But the cold is coming in.)

In my arms are strings, corpses, tables, sheets, but everything will be burned soon enough. All good things come to an end. All bad things too. You are dust, and you will return to dust. Dirty, sooty, dirty, mainly dirty, and even very dirty.

(The smoke is rising.)

Back then, when Mother closed the curtains and the doors, I would yell.
   When she gave me the key, I would yell even louder.

(The snow is infiltrating my shelter.)

When Father would come back from the woods, I would rediscover his face, which I had forgotten. As soon as he came in, he would pull Mother's hair and drag her to the bedroom.

(The floor is rumbling.)

And then once he didn't pull Mother's hair and didn't drag her to the bedroom. He looked at us and noticed me and my whiskers for the first time. He dragged me to the bathroom, grabbed the razor, and made his whiskers disappear into the sink. He held out the razor insistently for me to do to my face what he had just done to his.

(Chunks of ice are falling into the tub.)

Father left that night and never came back. Then Mother spent hours putting even thicker curtains on the windows.

(The roof is caving in.)

The storm may destroy my shelter. The Boots may be hot on my heels. Now I await only death, and I expect just one thing of it: that it be colossal.

IX

As I write this, the cabin is no longer standing. Every-thing disappeared in the storm. The window panes exploded, the walls came down. It was like at the movies: a big bang that takes everything with it. Then, darkness, worse than the darkness in my head.

Obviously, the world has been destroyed. The wind has the distinct taste of soil. The trees have been taken hostage, and animal fur litters the snow. Blood stains have settled on the snow. Some of what I have written has been scattered in the wind. It heads back down the forest trail, back to its origins. There are words everywhere, strewn everywhere, here, there, and yes, everywhere. Almost none left in my mouth.

The order of the indoors implodes. The order of the outdoors takes hold. Over there, my beloved Hare is deader than when he last died. His eyes are vacant, and his breath is gone. His body, his fur, and his spirit are no more.

And I haven't moved. I haven't moved my head, my body, my difference. I am still inside, while my body is outside. I remain in the shelter, but the shelter is no more. The wind is howling, and the forest looms, backlit. The snow piles up on the rocks in waves. I'm cold, but even so, I don't need walls to stay inside.

There is nothing left.

Nothing but me and my notebook.

I get up and walk through the rubble. I drag my feet and stir up the dust. I walk under the trunks, kick up stones. The cliffs hurl themselves into what looks like a void. Everything soils everything else.

Where will I find fire? Where will I find game? My feet slip in the snow. Around me there is only possibility. There is no clear road to take. All paths are open. Nothing but openings. Forks.

I advance. I hesitate. I fall. I lose blood, but it doesn't matter. A snout lies in the middle of a puddle, but it doesn't matter. A tongue juts out of the ground, but it doesn't matter. The earth puffs up its chest, trying to seem important.

The clearing leaves me as I leave the clearing. I head into the woods. I go where I don't belong. The earth groans with every movement; I tremble. Something has been broken in the earth. Not on the earth – in it.

I lurch. I fall. Gravity reminds me that I have a body. I see blood dripping from my head. My dress, which doesn't look like a dress anymore, billows. I fall again. I lift my head again, I get up again. Standing: facing the wrong way. Standing: continued incoherence. The bad weather is just a poorly written parenthesis that can be overcome.

I try to deal with the cold by tearing the bottom of my dress. I do my best to wrap my hands in the fabric. I'm cold. I'm cold.

I have one match left. If I strike it, will everything be okay?

Just one match left. The last one. I have to save it for the last moment. Am I there yet? Should I wait a little longer?

I spit on the ground. It's now or never. And I will rise to it like no one before me.

I strike the match against my sole and throw it onto the twigs. The fire struggles to catch. I give it some air. I fan it, and finally it crackles, it pops, it sizzles. I blow. The smoke rises. The heat lifts my dress and the flames along with it. Hot. Yellow. Orange. Red. Blue. Stained glass made of flames.

I lie down beside the fire and point my fingers to the ground. My lips taste like smoke. I whoop.

The clouds pass. Good.

The ground grows warmer. Okay.

The earth is turned over. Understood.

It's boiling under my hands. Perfect.

The ground is moving under my feet. Wonderful.

I barely have time to open my eyes, and the fire is spreading. I can still get up, but I don't.

Everything has to bing and bang for the end of the world and of me. First there is the fire. Then there is a grenade, but a life-giving grenade. Here, today, by the fire, I start a world war. Not the one being waged in the old countries, because there are actually lots of other wars taking place. Wars you don't see with the naked eye.

And that's what we need more of. We need insurgency. It needs to explode and unload – but in silence. Park the tanks, shut down the barracks, bring everyone back to the village. There is a new war on. You don't need to be called up to wage it.

The fire blazes its path by climbing into the trees. It melts rocks.

Take that, you bastard! Eat lead, swine. Die, die, like a crayfish out of water, mouth open, die! Everything that is dying should just die. Anyone who is considering suicide should just do it.

The fire is closing in around me. The smoke is choking me.

Then I remember the importance of saying a word every day with conviction: 'God.' So I say it: 'God.' I don't know whether my conviction is strong enough. I say it again: 'God.' Did that do it? To be sure, I say it again: 'God.' There, I've said it. That should do it.

Right now, at this very moment, I am immense. I feel the earth give way under my feet, and I sense that my movements keep the world turning. I put my hands over my ears, and all I hear is the hum of my body. I cup my hands over my nose, and all I breathe is the air of my lungs. My feet start to go faster.

From this point on, I will no longer be an animal, smaller and weaker. I have fire, so I have power. I don't care that my shelter was destroyed. I will build better cabins somewhere else. They won't be rundown hideaways in a nowhere swamp. They will be flawless, real, beautiful homes, built with a backhoe.

Triumphant, I stand up and turn on my heel. The fire is behind me, the shelter too. The ordeal is over. I am big and strong, like the Chic-Choc Mountains. I walk. The bellowing of things fills the space. The burning trees clutch at my body, flaming branches jostle my head. I push them away.

And I kick the ass of time.

And I advance.

And I keep advancing.

I want to reach the southernmost point where the caribou make their home.

I want to make a cave my home, unlearn language. I head down a hill, and rocks shift under my feet. The desire to run takes over. I run. I run.

This is not a simulation: I am an Indian. I know the

recipe for pemmican. I'm on an expedition. I'm heading toward the permafrost. This is an act of bravery, and it could cost me my life.

Once again I hear the muffled laugh of Mother, who would tug on my cheeks and braid my chin. I remember the grey paint I put on my face to blend in with the walls of my bedroom. The times when I would take refuge in Mother's arms so that she could smother me in her maternal folds. The doors always locked. I can see the muscular body of Father, who controls his stern impulses and allows me to play in the living room. I see knees being scraped. Trees disappearing. Soil piling up. I think about the colour that air would be if it were a colour. And I tell myself that this question cannot be answered, like so many others.

In a dream I see the pockmarked porch in soft wood. I walk toward Mother's house, and her back is turned to me. When I call out her name, she turns and stares at me. And I scurry toward the river.

But no matter.

I forget everything.

For good.

I start over.

For good.

The past is behind me, at rest.

Let it stay on its own, without me.

The last time that I did this or that no longer exists.
There is no last time anymore.
There is no first time anymore.
I let the present emerge.
It appears before me.
I let the past die.
It lives on its own.
And the present lives in me.
The past as sovereign.
The present is my yoke.

As I climb the mountain, the snow gets heavier and heavier. It buries me. God, I would like to have a snow blower, that modern machine they say is found in the cities. But I don't care about cities, and I don't care about gravity. Impassable, the Chic-Chocs? I beg to differ. The trees trip over themselves to bow before me; the tundra appears. I run into very little along this road up the mountain.

But a woodpecker stands before me.
I hadn't seen it. The clouds had obscured it.
My back arches.
My limbs stiffen.
Here I go …

And here is the finish line.

My dress stops billowing in the wind. I breathe in a single exhale. This pause is a retreat. I finally arrive at the end.

Far down below, the river. Beautiful, big, blue, gushing. With countless ice crusts. The waves keep breaking, never shutting their maws. And Anticosti Island, midway, in the distance, with its tribes of deer. And the rest of the Chic-Chocs, both pointy and rounded mountains, improbable geology.

I approach the edge. In the distance the water awaits me, because the tide is faithful to me. In the midst of the breaking waves, a trawler trawls no more. Nothing on the beach. Nothing on the docks. Unless … ?

I draw closer.

The ground slips from under me.

And I fall.

X

Lots of blood. Lots of pus. All I can see through my left eye is the wind twisting the trees, the scrawny trees, shredding them. I have bruises everywhere, even on my difference. All in all, it's disgusting.

I fell thirty feet. There's no way I can climb back up the hill. It hurts to breathe. I search for my breath as if it were hidden in the pit of my stomach. I moan. With each new breath, I die a little. The air dries the wounds on my head. I've felt better. A lot better.

Above the rock face, the burnt pine trees hold what remains in place. Their roots seem comfortable plunging into the void. This cave is a poor excuse for a shelter: it doesn't protect me from the night, the cold, or the weather. To convince myself that all is well, I smile an exaggerated smile. I widen my mouth as far as it will go, so wide that if anyone were to see me, they would worry for my jaw.

A thin trail of slime dribbles down the rocky walls. Frozen ivy dangles in it. My hands are lying behind my body, feeling the ground, scratching at the gravel. I can't fly, so I will hollow out a nest. My nails dig into the ground in hopes of hitting rock. I am looking for something that moulds to my woe, takes the shape of my captivity. All that binds me delights me: the stone cold of the ground, the black dust of the sandstone, the harsh humidity of the air.

I am pierced on the inside.

There is nothing on the ground, or under the ground.

Everything disappeared in the fire, at my hand.

The world died yesterday. Without a word of goodbye, without waving its hanky on the departure dock. It has breathed its last. It was bound to happen. I am the only one left alive. A quick glance at the horizon is all it takes to realize that I am the last thing the earth needs. Me who crawls so badly. Me who limps so well. Me who makes the ground recoil. When they see me, the dead trees bend and break.

These are not lies: the most complete revolution ever has just happened. I can say that because I have known both worlds: the old and the new. That's right, I lived through the transition. That's right, I have come a long way.

I mean, I am here. I am alive. Life is missing in action. I'm all there is left. Sometimes apocalypse leads to death but doesn't wipe everything out. Isn't witnessing the end of the world and surviving it where all the drama is?

Yesterday I was running away from the Boots, and today running seems pointless.

What do you do after the apocalypse? There are fewer options. Time drags on. Should I stretch out on nothing? Flop down nowhere? No. That would be depressing. Can I leave the cave? Wander through the remains? No, my legs can't walk anymore.

How long will I survive among the rocks? What is the point?

When you come right down to it, I liked being chased. When the Boots were looking for me, I was someone; with their violence came recognition. Now that they have stopped looking for me, do I exist? How do I know? How do I know myself? I can look at myself in the mirror all I want, but my eyes are the only ones doing the seeing. If no one is here to see me, am I really still here?

Ever since the apocalypse, the world has depended on me.

I am alone today. But maybe there will be someone else tomorrow. At the critical juncture of the apocalypse, can there be no after? An after-apocalypse? Or an after-after apocalypse? If someone suddenly appears tomorrow, they will know nothing of today or yesterday. The earth will have existed for no reason.

Unacceptable.

Unthinkable.

It is up to me to ward off this possibility by remembering everything.

It is up to me to be the world's witness.

On all fours, I clutch my pen and notebook. In the name of vertebrate heritage, I write. A killer whale washes ashore, a seagull heads straight for the steep river bank. Cod negotiate with whales. A school of lake trout struggles against a force, although I couldn't tell you which one.

I alone can inventory the extinct species. So I write. I write out loud. I write the Labrador duck, the pink-headed duck, the New Zealand thrush. I write the glaucous macaw, the Norfolk Island kaka, the desert kangaroo rat. I write the Sicilian dwarf elephant, the laughing owl, the Martinique giant ameiva. I write the northern curlew, the common red wolf, the European ass. I stand with the bubal hartebeest, the bush pig, the Atlas bear. I evoke the Tahiti sandpiper, the Réunion ibis, the spotted green pigeon.

And I yell: God! Why did you let them go?

Then the clouds burst. A mid-winter downpour. Heavy, cold rain melts the snow. It rains and it rains. It feels like the river will overflow and the water will rise to the mountaintops. Sad songs of the sea grab me by the throat. I don't hear them, but it is as if I did, because I hear a voice that tells stories of drunken sailors.

The water rises fast.

As high as my mouth.
As high as my nose.

Homo erectus. I stand up straight against the cave walls. I
cling to the roots as best I can. I keep my head above water.
The rock is high. I put my feet on it. I drag myself out of
the cave, where, by counter-miracle, it has stopped raining.

And I hear them.
    Yes.
    I hear them.
    A nasal honk.
    Deep.
    Like a lament and like a call.
    Honk. Honk. Honk. Honk.

Canada geese. Stunt flying. Formations.
    Spring is taking over the sky.
    They travel in spirant squadrons.
    Majestic.
    Enduring.
    Drawn by something that can't be seen.
    One in front, the others behind.
    The sound from their throats resonates through the
mountain.

And they disappear for a moment.

A long moment.

What if that was all that's left?

If another formation appears, I'll get up for good.

If another formation appears, it will prove that the animal kingdom is not done for.

If another formation appears, I will rebuild my life somewhere else.

Among them.

I am waiting for that formation now.

I am waiting, still.

I await it right now.

Still waiting.

And then birds appear in distinct shapes and sizes. Assembled with no regard for species, in a crescendo of cries.

Then in the distance, a shot.

XI

I abandon my cave for the safer heights of a willow tree. My arms grab onto whatever they can find. All over – and when I say 'all over' I mean 'all over me' – my sweat is tinged with the smell of bark. My fur bulks up. My fingers get caught up in the creeper, getting lost in it. I am so high that the wind blows harder and the air is drier and asteroids skim my head. Planet living is dangerous.

My eyes adjust to the light. I was right to say you can get used to anything. I've gotten used to the end of the world, its rebirth, and the return of the animals. Now that the end of the world is over, I am dreaming of another cabin. Walls, roof, window, door: I draw up the plans in my head. Soon I will reconquer the woods. But for now, I convalesce.

I do only one thing with my day: I gather snow to clean my wounds. It's disgusting, as I've said, but rubbing the skin makes it heal. Scabs form. At first, it's not like skin, then it becomes skin, at least skin as we humans know it.

Blood fills my throat, my nose, and my eyes. To say nothing of the pounding in my temples. Is it normal to burst out laughing? Is it normal to burst out vomiting?

You shouldn't move around too much when you are convalescing, but you shouldn't stay still when taking a leap into life either. So I try to stand up on the branches. I take off my shoes to feel the bark under my feet. I prefer when it pinches, when it tears. I stand up straight on my willow and rock back and forth. I must look strange.

I find two stones in my shoes. I rub them first in a clatter, then in the hopes of a concerto, finally to the beat of a requiem. I do it to warm up, but also out of my love of sound. It's hard to describe: I don't know many evocative onomatopoeias. They make a 'cling,' but a pure 'cling.' A completely pure 'cling.' My eyebrows arch as soon as I hear the sound. I can't believe that two stones can make this sound. I grab other stones, and my experiments confirm it: only these two stones, these exact two stones, produce the 'cling.'

That's enough.

I put the stones away and calmly consider the absence of game. I have been waiting for my beautiful animal for a few days. Ah! My beautiful animal. Stupendous. Wondrous. My stomach may be losing patience, but my spirit has hope. My chest is thumping wildly. I dream of venison, because I have eaten nothing but bark for days. It's bad, and I don't say that as a picky eater. I am a human being. My body needs to regain its strength. It needs nourishment from something other than bark.

So I imagine my animal, tall and slender, a female, with just enough muscle and refinement to allow itself to be devoured without carnage.

And I put myself in God's hands. If I put myself in the forest's hands, I would have to cry famine. There is nothing, absolutely nothing easily digested in this nowhere forest. I stare at my toes and wonder how long it would take to cook them to be edible. How would one prepare one's toes?

I write with my right hand, so my left hand is just an accessory. To hell with vanity. Should I bid it farewell? This delicious piece of me would keep the discomfort at bay. It would be good. It would get the job done: it would taste like pork, with a dash of pain.

As I think about the meal I could partake in both as diner and main course, something moves on the ground. I look down and knit my brows. I can make out a shadow, becoming increasingly clear. An animal, a bird.

A chicken. Yes, a chicken. Right there, more flesh than bone, a beautiful bird bowing its head. It is wandering and arching its back under my willow. It chirps, cackles, and clucks. I feel a pang in my stomach, and I salivate. Faced with this unlikely but edible creature, I spring into action: I set off after it.

The cedars, the birch, the beech: there is a whole forest to cross. I jump branch to branch. The wind tousles my hair. The needles lash at my arms. The branches plague my eyes. The pain is intense, but I keep moving, spurred on by my stomach. Chickens are faster than you would think. They can dart like nobody's business.

And then suddenly I lose elevation, I fall, I drop to the ground. I pick myself up and wobble a little. The animal runs off. I start walking again. My feet take off ahead of me. I follow closely behind.

Birds travel on the ground as in the air. They have wings on the ground, as in the air. My animal takes off even faster. I finally catch it. It gets agitated, fusses, resists. It makes a conspicuous face like it's the end of the world. It pecks at me and gets away, and runs and dashes and runs. Fleeting and unpredictable, it still has a weakness: it takes a break from its fate to eat gravel. Thank God for gravel.

Other chickens suddenly appear. A veritable banquet, it's practically Roman. They are different colours, even unexpected. They will have different flavours, even inde-scribable. I imagine a recipe: Light the fire. Place the chicken in a pot. Wash and chop vegetables. Season.

Cook over low heat for five hours. Set the table. Place the chicken on the table. Start with the legs. Move on to the breasts. Nibble the wings and the feet.

Before I cook them, I have to catch them. But how? I have no weapon or net or experience. I set snares for hares before Mother locked me in my room, but I know nothing of poultry. If only Father were here. Father, the elite hunter, would say, 'Don't think about the animal; think like the animal.'

So I stop thinking. The chickens are pecking like metronomes. I put my lips to the ground and eat gravel, too.

A crowing sound. Necks crane. Butts lift, and he makes his entrance.

Erect.

Massive.

He looks to be a foot and a half tall. His torso sticks out further than his chest. His wattle makes him so proud that he has to hide his face behind a mask. Otherwise if he looked at you, it would be too much.

He sees me.

He doesn't just sense my presence: he sees me.

The thing on his neck and the thing on my chin make us bellicose beasts. I hate him because he looks too much like me. I hate anyone who looks like me: they want to take my place in the world.

The rooster comes closer. I am taller than him, but he looks down on me. He puffs up more emphatically. Beats his wings. Spreads his disgusting odour over me. Sows his delicious, disgusting scent over me. Sprays his despicable, delicious, disgusting smell over me. I want to press my mouth against his body. I want to devour him. Put parts of him inside me. Out of love, I want to suck out his marrow and carry it inside me. Out of love, I look at his gentle eyes, which nauseate me. I arch my back. I shrink. Stare at me. Thrash me. Smack me around. My cheeks are soft, and my other cheeks are slightly furry. He brings his wings closer. Touches me. Grazes me. I go into his henhouse, he shoves me and closes the door.

I am locked up with the hens. It stinks of salmonella and feathers and straw and warm feelings. The rooster is there, perched way above, lording from on high, using the person that I am as a reference point. But am I really a person?

I can't reach the rooster. I can't offer myself to him. I can't take a bite of him. My face gets lost in a ballet of feathers and beaks. My desire is like that of the chickens. In the middle of this downy, white free-for-all, a scrawny bird rubs against my cheek. She slips between my legs, thinks I'm her mother. The chickens close ranks, huddle up, nip my cry in the bud. It's hot. It's stifling. Then it gets pleasant; we are comfortable, finally.

There are walls everywhere. The walls close in on me reassuringly. Rotten floors and rusty nails, with no trace of men. They must have been here once and now they are gone. All that is left here is feathers. Down. White.

I'm fed up.

I grab the rooster. I slip him under my dress and pull the drawstrings at the collar. He struggles and squawks. Ordinarily so authoritarian, now he looks like padding. He may lacerate my skin, set it ablaze, tear at the tissue, but he fights like a child. I can hardly believe he is credited with the dawn.

As soon as he moves, his skeleton hits my ribs. His little heart is thumping like mad. It must be love. Yes, this is what love must be. I think I am experiencing love. To love a rooster is to love an animal and to leave yourself open to rage and to renounce peace and quiet. Loving a rooster means loving savagely, embracing outrage, and daring to do yourself harm.

Squawks occasionally escape from my dress, so to the chickens, I seem like the boss. The chickens stay close to me, prepared to do my bidding. In a deep voice, I command them to honour me, to be beautiful and docile. Some of them lean against my calves. Others cluck saucy words. There will be no hanky-panky. I will not give in to your advances.

Tonight I will have a rooster to warm me. He is male. He is warm. I pull the ribbons of my dress tight so he can't escape. His beak hammers my breastbone. My breasts bleed. I have become a female, a real female. Suddenly I want to suckle something. Perform domestic tasks. I think about starting a family.

I close my eyes and fall asleep in the arms of a male.

But
    suddenly
    I am cold.

There is a big hole in my dress, and I am alone in my clothes.

Sounds of heavy footsteps reverberate outside. I shove the chickens aside, rush out, and spot the predator. He is tall, standing seven feet high. His mouth is bloody, and there are feathers in it. A comb. A beak. Wattle. The monster drops back down to all fours, and a booted man approaches him amiably. 'Good bear, Jo, nice bear.'

I drop to the ground. The dust, the moss, the lichen, the rocks, the feathers, the droppings, all of it gets in my mouth and the other holes in my face. I stifle a sneeze. I have to watch I don't suffocate. Am I properly hidden? I have doubts: the bear sniffs and turns his snout to me. I can't stay here a second longer. I crawl toward the forest, then I command my feet to do their thing and run without getting winded.

I escape before I'm noticed. A strong wind comes up. Luckily I know the Chic-Chocs, the secret passages, the way out. East to west by way of the north. You just have to find the main trail, then another after that. Turn right, left, right, and follow the river from there. Spend days roaming the forest. Don't be alarmed if you spot deciduous trees: the pines will return. They always return. Bear right, but not too much. Sneak a peek at the Albert Falls, then follow the traces of deer and moose in the vegetation. Howl to the east. Avoid falling into fifty-one traps. Don't think about tomorrow, because things could get worse.

My knowledge of things has convinced me: I will lose the bear, guaranteed.

XII

The cold mounts a new attack and slows my progress. I wish I could say I'm having a good time, but I'm not. I wish I could say that I'm smiling, but I'm not.

To hell with the rooster. I'm not a bird. I'm a mammal. I have mammaries, so it's only right that I fly this chicken coop. Mammaries aren't meant to be bitten by roosters, but by children and men.

It's horrible, when you think about it.

But life goes on.

My feet sink deeper and deeper into the snow. I rip a branch and pieces of bark from a pine tree. I attach them to my feet to make snowshoes. I want to make progress. It works, I'm advancing, but less efficiently than when I had nothing on my feet. So I take off my snowshoes. I tear down a hill, and what I see then makes my head spin.

Two tents in the valley and the smell of musk. It's a male. I can already make him out: plaid jacket, full beard. He is standing over the fire, a steaming mug in his hand, a gun slung across his back. He has a husky voice, like the voices of sailors lost at sea. My eyes linger on his shoulders, his arms, his angular hands. A scar runs down his neck. He has such a striking face that I want to name him: Clairmont.

Behind him is a black, restless shape, pacing. It's Jo, Jo the bear, chained, and suddenly I realize that the piece of meat cooking on the spit is a rooster: my rooster.

I feel sick to my stomach. The rooster no longer has a head, comb, or wattle. The stumps make him look ridiculous. He has lost what was glorious about him. He has lost what was wild about him.

If the Boots find me, they will kill me. They will start by cutting off my head. Then they will shave me, cut off my legs, and nail them to my arms. Is Clairmont wearing boots? Yes.

The ground is spinning so far off its axis that I lose my balance. I have to save the rooster. Animals are meant to be upright, not indolent and flopping about and well done on a spit.

Clairmont goes into the tent. His shadow is projected on the canvas. He lights a candle and searches through a bag. The coast is clear. With one eye on the tent and the other on the bear, I crawl toward the fire. I pull the rooster from the spit and stash it under my dress. I scramble toward the woods and dive behind a small hill.

The rooster is safe now. His crispy skin burns a layer of skin off my torso. The dripping fat relieves the shooting pain. I take a look down my dress: he has lost all of his plumage. He is just a damaged golden body with a tantalizing smell. He doesn't move or struggle to escape from my tattered dress. I run my fingers over his skin and daintily sniff them. I rub the fat over my lips. My teeth delicately attack the meat. Bite by bite, I ingest strips of skin. I swallow. I sob. I swallow. I sob. Rest assured, rooster, I'm not getting rid of you. I will keep your bones in my pocket.

'Oh for chrissake! The chicken. The chicken is gone!' A man with red hair comes out of his tent and waves his arms around. His fat swings from left to right, and a trail of dirty liquid has stained the front of his shirt. Authority gushes from his mouth. Clairmont comes out of the tent and drops his pot. He grabs Red by the throat: 'Where were you?' They are men of few words. They remind each other of the importance of staying near the fire to watch for thieves. They use words like *selfishness, greed, trickery, laziness*, as if they were urgent topics of conversation. Finally, Red, the larger of the two, loads his gun and heads into the woods, grumbling, 'This is between him and me.'

He heads toward me, walks by the bushes I am hiding in. Sweat, piss, curdled milk: his scent fills my nostrils. His steps seem as heavy as the bear he holds prisoner. I haven't come around to the idea that he is a hunter: he is so fat, big and fat. His boots brush my feet. He keeps his head up and doesn't see my face hidden behind the branches. *Pow! Pow!* He slings his shotgun over his shoulder, grabs a red animal, and carries it back to the camp. Bloodied but alive, the fox moans.

Clairmont makes fun of him. 'You actually think that fox stole the chicken? There isn't a piece of meat left on the spit, and the spit is still there. He went to the trouble of sliding the chicken off it and then putting the spit back. No, it can't be him. A hunter, yes, an Indian, definitely, a ghost, maybe … but not a fox. Let him go back to the forest. He is paying for someone else's crime.'

Red rubs his face: 'You don't know anything about foxes. And anyhow, he's going to die. It's better this way.'

Clairmont gets up and picks up a can. 'It's not much for two, but it's better than nothing.' He opens the tin and pours the baked beans into a pot, which he places over the fire. 'I told you we should have stayed longer in the village to get supplies.' While Clairmont feeds the fire, Red is lost in thought. His eyes widen: 'Hey, you'll laugh but … what if it was Rose-Marie's daughter who stole it? If you ask me, she didn't get very far. What if she stayed in the area after she went missing? We would get a big reward if we found her.' Clairmont drops his spoon in the pot, strokes his beard for a moment, and starts laughing: 'Ha ha! One week alone in the woods in mid-March? No way. She wouldn't survive. She isn't cut from the same cloth as her father. Courage is handed down father to son, never father to daughter.' After exhaling, he goes on: 'What with the storm two days ago, I wouldn't count on it. You don't survive that sort of thing in the forest, particularly at that age. If you want to know what I think, Rose-Marie shouldn't have locked her away like that. Those sorts of stories always end badly.' Red doubles over, laughing: 'Ha ha! Rose-Marie was the one who should have been locked up, not the kid. The mother may be good-looking, but she's not all there.'

Calling Rose-Marie crazy isn't nice. And it says so in books: you need to respect your elders, particularly when you are close-knit. And I left the village a month ago, not a week ago. I know how to count mornings. I am an accountant.

No, the hunters aren't talking about Mother and me. Rose-Marie is a common name: there is the nightclub singer, the herb, and others.

Yes, that's it. The hunters must be talking about another Rose-Marie. Even if it's not certain, it's okay. You can never be sure of anything. There are so many unanswered questions. Does God talk? Where is space? What comes first, day or night? Why is there bedtime? What happens if you don't sleep? Can animals count? Why are there nail clippings in the world? When we die, do we become a ghost of an old fart or a silhouette of a young filly? Yes, the hunters are talking rubbish.

Red adds: 'Do you remember when Jo refused to eat moose? You had to beat him with a hot iron to get him to swallow a piece.'

I can smell the booze all the way over here, and the men are getting comfortable. Clairmont unbuttons his jacket and opens a bottle. 'I didn't try to beat him to death though.'

The men watch the fire in silence. One minute, two minutes. Clairmont is emphatic: 'You have no idea how much I am looking forward to getting out of the woods and being with a warm-blooded woman again. To settle in between her thighs and her breasts. And fuck her.'

This time, no throaty laugh. The men are looking for something to dispel the emotion and make them laugh again. 'And to think you thought it was Rose-Marie's daughter, Christ. It reminds me of the time that Indian woke us up. Do you remember? He was old … '

The stories continue and spread through the forest. Powerless, I let them fill my head just before I fall asleep, alone with others, behind the hill.

XIII

The day caught me unawares. The embers have died. The men have left the camp, but their tents are still there. The tracks on the ground show them heading east. They will be back. But not right away.

I take advantage of the hunters' absence to approach Clairmont's tent. On the ground, there is a pallet and a blanket with masculine motifs. Sleep has permeated the fabric. I inspect the seams, inventory the curly hair, count the slivers of skin. I plunge my nose into the pillows.

Suddenly, the smell. My hair is a mess, and I can't think about anything else. It smells so good that I have thoughts of marriage. My lips drop to the sheets. It smells like man and effort, musk, muted aggressiveness. What if I have just met my man?

I put on the red hunting jacket and stick my hand in the right pocket. I find a penknife. In the left, a razor. On a little pendant, a miniature version of Jesus Christ our Saviour watches over the tent. I hang a souvenir of my rooster on the leather string it dangles from, a tiny bone. Then I spot the unthinkable: a chocolate bar, untouched. I unwrap it and breathe in the smell. I bite into it, and the flavours explode. I eat it all, all, all, except for a small piece that I save for later.

My investigation continues. In a grey canvas bag there are books, brushes, and photos. I see Clairmont posing with a white sturgeon. I admire Clairmont in the woods and the ocean. Clairmont celebrating a victory in the forest, and then, a large group of males representing the full spectrum of hairiness. In front of the group, a bear with its tongue hanging out, killed on site. The sun was bright that day: they are squinting. It's what is called 'having the sun in your eyes.' Only one is looking straight ahead, eyes wide. His big nostrils take up much of the photo. An athlete's jaw juts outs from under a thick beard. His muscular hands hold an axe. If he had wrinkles, he would look like Father. But it's Clairmont.

Suddenly there is nothing: nothing left to eat, nothing left to see, nothing left to do. It all happens as if the silence has been turned up and the noise has been turned down. The tent smells good, but I have seen all there is to see. There are no more crannies to explore, no more stray crumbs. I feel like someone who has done it all and who is disappointed at having succeeded at life. Succeeding means achieving and achieving means finishing; only the imperfect life is worth living.

The rattle of Jo the bear's chains brings me back to reality. I have to get away from the Boots. I can hear them. The men are stumbling back. Alcohol is interfering with their gait. I grab the burlap sack and stuff things into it. I grab the pictures of Clairmont (not all the pictures, because every man is entitled to a few memories), I hug the musky pillows one last time and scramble out of the tent.

I climb back up a tree to get some perspective on life. The fire crackles. A can is partially opened and releases the smell of beans. Once again, the men take their places in the camp. Clairmont shuffles cards for a few seconds. Cards are made for playing, and he shuffles them: he is so adorable!

Red heads toward Clairmont's tent. He goes in and yells: 'For chrissake!' Clairmont joins him. He sees that he's been robbed. The men scuffle, swear at each another, accuse each other. 'You took the bag, you sonofabitch.' 'No, you took it.' 'Dammit! Even the pictures are gone.' 'Ah, don't worry about it! The pictures weren't even that good. They didn't look like me. I look much better now.'

I'll admit it for the sake of my soul: anxiety tied a knot in my stomach. Stealing a man's memories is risky business. God forgive me, for posterity! God protect me, by the hair of my chinny chin chin! Reconciled, the men hastily arm themselves and scout the area. They are after revenge. They are two big, dirty men. All I have to defend myself is my tree. I am at the very top, frozen. I hope I blend in with the bark. I hope my pursuers have bad eyesight. Being pursuers, they do what they have to do: they pursue me.

They spot tracks on the ground. An owl screeches. They are afraid. They are trembling. Their armour and metal buttons are clanging. 'It's Big Chief,' Red says, 'the Indian we shot last year. He said he would be back.' The men return to the camp, pack their things, and head into the woods. They aren't very seasoned hunters. They lose their nerve fast.

Thrusting my hands into the burlap bag, I find a tiny object: a mirror. I observe half my face, bearded, with the plaid shirt. And this time I think of Father. I would look a lot like him, I think, if I resembled him and had his features. Just like him.

I will watch over the sleep of the two big fat guys like a father should.

XIV

I spot a great expanse of ice to the west. It's a lake, and not just any lake: it is one heck of a lake. Judging from the circumference, I conclude that it must be home to many fish: herring, cod, pike, smelt, halibut. It's been a while since my last meal: I ran into the hunters two days ago. And now they are off on an expedition to the middle of the forest.

Since I no longer have the sight of two beautiful males to entertain me, I decide to come down out of the tree and do a bit of ice fishing. I don't go alone: I am flanked by my rooster, even though he is as quiet as quiet can be hanging on the string around my neck.

First we make our weapon: a harpoon. We find the branches we need, and we get out our penknives – actually, I'm the one who does it on my companion's behalf. We plant our blades in the bark. We cut fangs from the trees.

It is the exacting work of a master, but as luck would have it, we are no longer babies. At our command, the branches reach out, get tangled with each other, and break. There: our weapon is built. We are ready to fish.

We head into the grey forest. Left, right, left, right. We walk in single file and make noise to scare off the animals. We let them know who is in charge. We give them proof, indisputable proof. By making improbable noises, we show them that the trail belongs to us. Even when they answer, we don't tremble, or at least not much. I hold the harpoon nice and straight on my companion's behalf. I will throw it if I have to, in the direction of fur grown too curious.

The path becomes clearer, and the forest closes in. The spruce bow: their needles dilate, swell. The phalanxes, middle phalanxes, and distal phalanxes of the branches whip our face. On the right, I watch out for roots and rocks: one fall and down we go.

You can hear the oaks groan. Winter has sucked up all the light. The air is so dense that the thickets huddle to catch a breath. A stream burbles against a thin layer of ice. In the highest treetops, bird skeletons dangle head down.

Panting reaches us from afar. Then barking. Mad. Discordant. The smell of a massacre tracks us like a shadow. Tufts of fur flutter in the leaves, and our legs distance themselves from each other.

He appears, straight ahead. Two tons of black fur, sharp claws, and pointy fangs. He stands on his hind legs and growls. It's cliché, but it's really what he does at this very moment. Jo, Jo the bear. A chain around his neck, but loose.

'Quit showing off!' I tell him. 'Jo, we know you're not mean.' But Jo keeps it up, won't let the joke die. He keeps pretending to be a ferocious animal. He roars, bares his fangs, claws at the ground.

What are a few words from a woman worth in the face of a two-ton powerhouse? He managed to escape for a reason, the big teddy. I close my hand around my pendant and repeat that the joke has gone on long enough. Jo comes closer. His mouth opens even wider. His big mouth open like a cathedral. A mouth so wide open that he could shove me in it. I stand up tall on my heels. Jo does the same, but this time he takes a moment to place a claw against my cheek.

A machine gun goes off in my head. I spit, I bark. I recite all of God's names in a single breath.

Jo backs up. One step, two steps, three steps. Looking deflated and sad, he licks his paw and moans. His head and his body sway; he shakes his paws and rattles his chains. Jo won't take his eyes off mine. He won't take his eyes off my cheeks. He won't take his eyes off my beard.

What is a big ol' bear to do when everyone thinks he is bloodthirsty? The question niggles at him. For a horrible beast, he has gentle eyes. Maybe I remind him of Father, a beard by trade. Maybe one day Father was kind to him. Maybe he offered him apples and berries in a grand gesture of generosity.

Like a pet dog that has been locked up for too long, Jo is bored. His instinct doesn't know which paw to shake anymore. He gnaws at the corners of the table, chases his own tail. Jo doesn't know how to be wild anymore. He looks for easy prey, but he has lost his sense of drama.

You just have to see his vacant eyes and slumped shoulders to feel pity for him. Yes. I feel genuine emotion for Jo. Yes. I sympathize. He and I are cut from the same cloth. Chains have branded our character.

Come to think of it, maybe we could join forces. We could disrupt the human race, probably better than anyone. Derail it and set it off down a new track. Yes, this is our goal now: to recreate the human race. Steer it toward what it is not, uproot it, disrupt it. Not annihilate it forever, but create competition, a parallel species that instills a bit of fear. A species identical in appearance (stands upright, fires neurons) but, oh, so much better. A species next to which men will be ashamed to stand.

Jo hides his intentions well, because he still hasn't budged. He is so happy being unhappy that he has stopped sharing his pain with me. Between sighs, he unearths a rope from the ground. His claws get caught up in it, and soon, he is holding the rope with a firm paw. He closes his eyes for a bit and, finally, turns his back and gives it a good yank.

I've barely lifted my head when a net falls on me. Two men in boots with a familiar scent clamber down from the trees. They are everywhere: their biceps rest on my head, their abdominals press against my legs, their shoulder blades hit me in the stomach, their big fingers drive into my back.

Then their net closes around me. I can't get my arms or feet out. The big fat men lift me up and chuck me in a cold, square space. A stony creak seals my fate: I am thrown in the clink.

They finally got me, the Boots.

XV

They carry me like two proper males should, on their big fat shoulders. I am dangling in mid-air from a branch in a prison of metal and wood. They are saying it is a solid cell, a suitable dungeon for a beast like me.

Wily beast that I am, I won't let them do whatever they like. If they think they are going to carry me like this until the end of the story, they are sorely mistaken. I shout myself hoarse, I show my fangs, I spit, I growl. My arms slice through the air. I make the cage swing left and right, I throw my body up against the sides. The men make fun of me: 'A nice catch, and stubborn too!' They comment on my teeth, the length of my nails, the chubbiness of my cheeks. 'A catch like this is going to bring in some money. A lot more than pelts.' When Red comes close to my face, I turn and show him my rounded back, my fur bristles, and I make a shrill sound. The men jump back, slapping themselves on the thighs. They are laughing.

We head back through the forest in the opposite direction. Spruce branches brush against me, but I'm in no mood to greet them. To slow the march I grab the needles with all my might. I shout, 'Back, back, back!' but the men just have to move the cage along for the forest to slip through my fingers.

The clearing reappears. The camp is still set up. The men stoke the fire: a plump partridge awaits them. They put Jo beside me, and he immediately starts sniffing me every which way, through any means possible, from every angle.

The men attack their meal in a chorus of slurps. They hold out a piece of meat to me. When I try to grab it, they pull it back and grin. I growl. Clairmont's fingers approach me. A mild smell, sour and musky. I breathe it in, closing my eyes, I imagine my body lying next to his and my fingers running through his beard. Then I come back to my senses and growl again. Treason! Treason! High treason!

As the smell of the fire hangs in the camp air and the night grows thicker, thoughts infect the men who normally don't think. 'I was wondering: do you think we should take the road west or head directly to the ridge?' Clairmont swallows his mouthful, wipes a dribble of fat off his forearm, and says, 'The kid is heavy. It's going to be hard to take the shorter road. What I'm worried about is supplies.

There's not a lot of hunting once we're on that road. Do you think we have enough food for the four of us?' Red furrows his brow. 'The four of us? You're counting her too?' Clairmont throws the old bear a piece of the partridge, which he gulps down. 'We don't have a choice. They want her alive. But don't worry. We won't give her anything until she settles down.'

I shout even louder. 'You can keep your murderer's meat!' I don't need food to survive. There are plants that can live for hundreds of years in a bottle with no water. They are self-sufficient. They have a bit of light, and they create their own ecosystem. When you have nothing in this world, you just have to create your own ecosystem.

I keep yelling. I stop only to catch my breath. The outer edges of my body give way; I am overflowing on all sides. My voice starts getting hoarse, and my throat burns. But I keep it up. I go at the sides of the cage again; my teeth grind against the bars. To make the racket stop, the big fat guys will have no choice but to set me free. Clairmont comes closer to observe me carefully. 'I've trapped a lot of wild animals in my life, but never one like this. She's been in the cage for three hours, and she still hasn't given up. Too bad we have to hand her over to the village. She would make a fine hunting trophy.'

Village. My fate becomes clear in a word. That's where they're taking me. I have to figure out how to get away, no matter what. I would have resigned myself to being roasted on a spit like my rooster. But being burnt at the stake like a heretic, while the villagers look on, I cannot abide.

I slip my hands into my pockets. The razor is still there. I've read enough Westerns to know what to do. I just have to file the bars with the blade, and they will give way. I'll wait for night before I start.

'Will you look at that. Suddenly the little beast is quiet. Why have you stopped shouting? Cat got your tongue?' The men look at each other and beam. The combined effect of the silence and time passing makes their muscles go slack, and they slump down on the logs. With heavy arms, they pull out a bottle from their bag. As they tell hunting stories, they pass the bottle back and forth. The alcohol goes to their head, glory too: 'I'm going to shave before we get to the village. Women like a smooth cheek. When they see the reward our beast brings in, they'll be throwing themselves at us.' The swigs grow longer and so does the silence. Heads bob and the men go to their tents.

They breathe heavy, they breathe dry, they are already snoring. The coast is clear. I get out the razor blade and start filing the bars. It makes a scraping sound. The bear jumps. I hide the blade under my dress. I have to be prudent and destroy my shackles with caution. My hands start moving again.

The cage is still in one piece. There is barely a scratch on the metal bars even after several minutes. I yawn. My eyes close. I yawn again. My eyes close again. I slip the razor into my pocket and lay my head down on the floor. Will I escape tomorrow? It remains to be seen.

XVI

The morning glowers. The men noisily break camp. They are using drums and trumpets, banging pots, and swearing vociferously. Their objective is to get the hell out of here. For them it is a march toward glory. For me it is a forced return to the seaweed, Christ on the cross, and the pealing bells. They want to return my body to the world, to put an end to my flight. My throat constricts at the very thought.

The males grab everything they can. A pile of things hang from their shoulders. They tie the rest to the bear, who seems oblivious to his role as porter. Every person carries a house on their back. They have what they have because they are strong enough to have it. If their muscles atrophy and they can't carry some of it anymore, they have to return it to nature.

For now, they can keep me in captivity because they are strong enough to carry me. That means that my hope of being released into the forest is directly proportional to the amount of food I ingest. Give me something to eat and drink! I have a reputation as an ogre to forge.

Exhausted, the men hitch a cart to the bear. They put my cage on it so they don't have to carry it. My prison can no longer be toppled. It would make a terrible racket, and they would catch me before I got away. Plus, the cart is shaking too much for me to start filing the bars. I will have to think of another way to get out of this pickle. I try to think, but I don't think. Thinking is for the free.

I fumble in the bottoms of my pockets. I find the small mirror. I see part of my cheeks. The whiskers God gave me come with responsibility. The idea of returning to the village led by two other beards is revolting.

The bear lifts its snout to the sky, and, with the way he is drooling, I realize that he is not doing it for fun. Clairmont has a piece of meat in his bag that is starting to smell. As the aroma builds, I grow certain that the only way to earn an animal's trust is to tame his stomach with the promise of a meal. At any given moment, Jo could sink his teeth into Clairmont's neck. But he doesn't, in the hopes of eating more and better because of him.

'A bowl of pea soup. Fresh homemade bread. A big hunk of cheese. The waitress's green eyes and a couple of beers. Just think of how delicious it's going to be to go home,' Red says.

Hearing him list his fantasies, I have an idea, the very one I need. The words take shape in my mouth in a long series of whispers. 'Jo, my ally in adversity, you're hungry, aren't you? It's no fun eating nothing but beans. Wouldn't you love a nice hunk of meat with raspberry sauce? Wouldn't it be nice to sink your teeth into the meat and the sugar? Free me, and I will free you in turn. We could hunt together, and I would feed you apple pies. We would eat blueberries until we were ready to burst. Imagine the forest and the animals we could devour. These aren't lies. I'm not just whispering sweet nothings in your ear. We would steal a cow from a farm and have milk and butter.' With a stab of regret, I take out my last piece of chocolate and throw it to the bear. He bends down, his eyes grow wide, he sniffs the chocolate and then eats it. He slows down. Clairmont turns and yanks on the bear's chain. He jumps ahead, his head bowed.

'Oh, Jo, poor Jo, my companion in misery, you can't let yourself be defeated like this. You are a wild animal. You are fearsome. You have claws and fangs. God didn't give them to you for knitting. You shouldn't be so agreeable, so civilized. You could rip off your tormenters' heads with just a swipe of your paw. Their words and their axes are like lace next to your weapons. Break your bonds. Together, we can give them the beating of a lifetime.'

My sales patter has no effect. Jo continues to obey his assailants. His paws sink into the ground. His mouth is filled with stifled roars. His growls smell musty. He likes his chains. Every time Clairmont yanks on the shackles that hold him, Jo closes his eyes, savouring the violence he has fallen victim to. Oppression calms him. He is like a child who has misbehaved and who feels pacified by a spanking. Basically, this big, tough guy finds freedom terrifying. If his shackles were removed, he would be forced to find food himself. There would be no fire to warm him. There would be no hand to pet him.

Tough! If I can't grumble outside my cage, I will grumble behind the bars. Why go to all the trouble of escaping when I can settle into myself? No one can stop me from settling into myself. I retreated in my shelter; I can retreat in this jail, with the others looking on.

I know that this will require a serious inner flight: I have to close my eyes and head into the darkness. I have to suppress all stimuli that could cause my eyes to fly open. Avoid surprise, banish fear, forget the movement that is taking me back to the village. Concentrate on my breath, my pulse, my gurgling. It is up to me to impose my own rhythm again. It is up to me to decide how quickly the fecal matter moves through my guts. The inner music won't come on its own. I have to make it come, then, when it is firmly present, forget that I conjured it to complete the illusion.

The men are still getting ready to leave. They resume their assault by imposing themselves from the outside. Their smell seethes from them. They yell, piss, and shit. They spread their scent through the forest. I have to retreat from them. Escape, settle into myself, and take a look at my own eyes directly, but it is difficult with all the noise.

I find my centre again. The men walk, and I don't care. I put down roots in the cage. It pitches to the left; it pitches to the right. I remind myself that I'm not alone. I press up against my rooster to ward off nausea. An inner landscape emerges. We will reach the body of water for phenomenal fishing. We will reach the beast with the silver back: the marlin.

There is no need to wait any longer: the lake is there, immense, in front of us. It is covered with a thin layer of snow, like icing sugar. If we scratch a little and brush aside the snow, we might find goldfish. The rooster seems famished. 'No,' I tell him, 'those fish are just for decoration.' Here we fish the monster of the sea, the fish of legend: the marlin.

Here we go. The cage is gone, so are the hunters. We are winter sailors, and our boat is the ice field. We scrape the snow from the ice. We just need to follow the biggest shadow to determine the exact location of the prey of our dreams. Once we have spotted the shadow, we make a hole in the ice using a harpoon and a penknife. Shavings of cold swirl in the wind. The water eventually bubbles up from the hole.

Heeding the advice of the rooster, which doesn't have much to say as a little bone hung around my neck, I tear off a bit of my dress and put it on a hook. I will use it as bait. Drop my line into the water. You have to keep jiggling it, otherwise it freezes. Time passes. And there are little tugs on the line. 'Go on, eat, eat until the hook pierces your cheek. I'll pull you up without any fuss, and that will be the end of your life and the start of your death.'

There is a tug on the line. The fish is a fighter. I try to pull it toward me.

'Just four more kilometres, big guy, and we'll be back in Rivière-à-Pierre.'

The men's voices come back to the fore.

The marlin line is broken.

I close my eyes again. I focus on the darkness.

No, it isn't winter anymore.

It isn't winter anymore, it's summer. I'm older: I am fifteen, and Mother is sleeping on the ground. She has flowers in her hair. When she joins me on the beach, I notice that her breath smells like licorice. I want to stick my tongue in her mouth to taste it, too. She leaves me on the beach and goes back to the river. I struggle to walk to her, I stumble, fall in the water, and the salt fills my nostrils. The rocks in the river turn fascinating colours; I get closer to touch them: floral white, Persian blue, electric indigo, kelly green, lobster red, grape. 'None of those colours existed in my day,' Mother says.

I am sixteen. My breasts are heavy. The air is warm. I am tall and slim. My hair brushes the ground like a wedding dress. There is a crown of vines on my head. The wind makes my dress billow. Everything smells like jasmine candy.

A man is wearing boots. When he walks, and he walks a lot, he lifts his knees up high. He doesn't smile and never takes his eyes off the ground. The seagulls return to line up along the dock. The fishermen are busy with their nets and hauling traps. The man walks alone, eyes firmly on the clean boots he is wearing. The humidity has gotten into his hair. And this time, only this time, no one knows why, the man raises his head. He doesn't focus on anything, but he sees me. I'll admit I don't hate it.

Rivière-à-Pierre stretches out behind him. I see the village again, not as I know it, but as it could be in the best of all possible worlds. And as I think of it now, it contains everything, all at once: apple trees, rose bushes, snowy roads, wooden crosses, iron crosses, cross my heart and hope to die, churches, candy, summer days, days when we tell ourselves we are going to have a good day, days when we tell ourselves it couldn't be better, days when we wait impatiently for night, nights of yesteryear, starry nights,

nights when we escape humanity, nights when we eliminate humans, the state in which we live when we stop depending on men, the beginning of the disappearance of men, the initial decomposition of bodies, the advanced decomposition of bodies, what will remain of human bodies in eleven hundred and eleven years, what will remain of me in eleven hundred and eleven years, what will remain of Rivère à Pierre in eleven hundred and eleven years.

Nothing.

In eleven hundred and eleven years, nothing will remain of Rivière-à-Pierre as I know it today, so why fight it?

So I try to see the village as it is. I accept the men, the cosmos and its manifestations. I tolerate the starless nights and put up with bad weather, boredom, illness, mockery, wounds. I accept the moment when Mother locked herself away in silence, the moment when at eleven years old I wanted to live in a black hole, in two black holes, in three black holes, in four black holes, in five black holes, in six black holes, in seven black holes, in eight black holes, in nine black holes, in ten black holes, in eleven black holes.

Suddenly I can put up with anything. The world is at once inside me and outside me. There is no point trying to tear myself away from my inner world. I don't need to look within to see clearly. The world is there, within my grasp. I just need to break my bonds to reach it. I have built this prison within. It's up to me alone to escape from it.

In a moment, I will let the light and the sounds submerge me. In a few seconds, I will let the outside in. I will raise the white flag and let myself be invaded by the light of day. I needn't be afraid. I just have to let myself be carried away for a moment or longer, as the case may be.

First I hold my breath. One second, two seconds, three seconds, four seconds. (It is so nice in here.) Five seconds, six seconds, seven seconds, eight seconds. (Will I be able to go back?) Nine seconds, ten seconds, eleven seconds, twelve seconds.

I miss the air.

And I give in.

XVII

Waking up knocked me senseless. My mind is bathed in sweat, on alert. My eyes are tired of being closed. I try to turn my eyeballs toward the optical nerve, but nothing works. Every time I move my eyes I want to scream. A scream projected outward, therefore outside of me.

The world of men is sticky, soft, and heavy. Their bellies hang over their belts; their mouths spew words in bold. The animals howl, and the men shoot. All around me, animals line the trail and gnaw on fresh meat. They eat so much that they have to keep crouching for relief. Bursts of light appear. I take them in the eye, even closed.

'It's okay. You can take me to the village.' The hunters turn and look at me with contempt. 'Take me to the village,' I demand. Clairmont gets up and kicks my cage: 'What are you talking about? Why aren't you shouting?

We didn't mind you shouting.' I turn up the silence. One, two, three minutes. It is not easy to back down from two musky men. 'Take me to the village. Since I must, I'll make myself pretty and be as docile as a pebble.'

A dramatic turn. Not a word is spoken, but an argument breaks out. Red unhooks the cage from the cart, puts it on the ground. The men step away. Jo looks at me, bored, hunger in his belly. He growls and whimpers at the same time. He doesn't know whether he should swallow me whole or sympathize with my captivity. If he steps so much as one paw toward me, it's all over.

I hear the hunters' raised voices in the woods. They spit my animal name rather than speak it in human language. They can't agree. They talk about money, honour, shame. They shove each other, brandish their weapons. The forest comes alive. The men push each other around. Then silence. The strongest has won.

The march continues, slower and slower. They have poured lead in their boots. They stumble over the smallest of twigs. Nothing is said, but my voice echoes in their heads. When they pitch camp at the end of the day, the silence is at full volume. The men know that the village is just a few hours' walk away and that the moment when I will be unveiled to the world is nigh. Sleep won't come. Clairmont and Red's minds are filled with thoughts.

I have an idea.

When I was little, I wouldn't let sleep take me by surprise. I preferred to fall asleep on my own terms. Rather than letting the darkness carry me off into slumber, I would stay awake all night. During the day, with my head against the window, I would let the sun shine in my eyes, I would tell myself stories and fall asleep in the afternoon. I still like telling myself stories.

So here is a short one, recent and highly rhythmic, to tell to two real men who can't sleep: 'Once upon a time, in a nearby forest, there were two big, fat, smelly hunters. One had a brown beard, the other had a red beard.'

Abrupt movement in the tents. Weapons in hand, the two men poke their heads out and stare at me.

'They smelled so deliciously despicable that someone nicknamed them the skunks of the woods. They had been roaming the forest for days looking for uncommon prey. Deer, moose, bear, and cougars had caught their attention, but none of them were legendary enough to deserve the honour of death by bullet. They were looking for something rarer. They wanted to write a page of Chic-Chocs history.'

Weapons pointed to the ground. Mouths open, passive, the men listen to me, their muscles taut.

'They had spent days sparing lives, and their wallets were growing thinner. They were about to go back to the village empty-handed when they spotted, in a hollow of the woods, a beast not common in these parts. The animal was beautiful, but her fury and her voice were even more compelling. As they approached, the men saw that their prey stood no more than five feet high, creating a curious contrast with the ogre's cry that came out of her mouth. The animal was struggling like the devil in holy water. Her tiny fangs chopped through the air; her paws and claws tried to grab anything that moved. For days, the forest denizens could not sleep, so deafening was the noise. The melody of the birds could no longer be heard in the morning. The two men congratulated each other on their catch. Pride was getting the better of them.

'But it is dangerous, very dangerous to keep a wild animal in a cage for too long. As the days went by, the beast stopped her racket; her fury was spent. Myth gave way to the everyday, even boredom. From the wild animal she was, the creature became a pet. Docile. Accommodating. Should they bring her back to the village? The villagers would not be the least bit surprised by the catch. Instead, they would burst out laughing at the men who were proudly displaying her.'

Clairmont gets up. His body is wracked with spasms. His lips sealed tight in rage. He rips branches from the scraggly trees. He shreds ferns. His boots try to gain traction. After stomping around, they collide with a stump. He takes a pot out of a bag, shakes it in my direction. He scrutinizes my face with his big eyes, lets his jaw go slack, and howls. I don't move a muscle. He yells out names I have never heard before. His face comes close to mine in an endless to and fro. He orders the bear to attack. Jo doesn't so much as twitch. Clairmont lifts the cage and hurls it at a tree trunk. Red watches him impassively, as if he can't take in the drama playing out before his eyes.

I don't move a muscle. I don't say a thing. I don't even furrow my brow. Clairmont yells: 'Scream, howl, defend yourself! Wave your paws, show your fangs!' I curl up in a ball, partially hide my face with my hands, and smile.

A cry is heard in the forest. Fists balled, chest out, Clairmont tries to contain his rage. Words turn soft in his mouth, his eyebrows relax. First his violence is stifled, then it is no longer violence at all. He sits down, plunges his thick fingers into his beard. His shoulders slump.

The moon ends its journey through the sky, and my vocal cords prefer to take no further action.

XVIII

The cage is open. Light snow erases the tracks on the ground. Even using my nose, I can't track the smelly bear. The big fat men have left. They have moved their tents, their provisions, their curse words. If they have strength and instinct, they will train Jo to attack them. They will return to the village bloody, their flesh wounded, and arouse sympathy. They would have a story to tell, even with no prey.

The world is right there, in front of me, within my reach. One muscle at a time, I rediscover the weight of my body, re-experience my fingers, my knees, and my legs. I feel tingling when I set my limbs back on the ground. Pages fall onto the snow, carried by the snowflakes. My writing has followed me here.

I propel my body and its thoughts forward. My right hand initiates the movement. My arm follows it, then my shoulders, torso, and legs obey in turn. I crawl in the cold.

It's hard to regain your balance as a human after having been an animal for days.

The hunters took pity on me. They left all the wool clothing they had: a scarf, a toque, and mittens. Layer by layer, they undressed. Arm by arm, extremity by extremity, phalange by phalange, I insert myself to the very end of the fabric. Dressed like this, feeling small, I go through the door. All of the outside enters me.

The world is restarting.

There is no more inside, only outside. The cold nips at my cheeks, infiltrates through my nostrils, which freeze immediately. I cough and spew the icy air outside. Now that I am standing, the snow squeaks under my feet. I have to start moving, but I fall.

The wind blows furiously and pins my legs to the ground. I have to turn my head to breathe. Stalactites hang from my eyelashes. I hurl myself forward, and the gusts push me back. I wait for the wave to recede. The snow charges to the ground. It sticks to it like glue.

I dream of a box I could be locked in.

No. I have to get up. Again. Yes, that's it, I get up. Another push – if the earth is willing. But I soon stumble – the earth is not willing. Maybe I should abandon my journey in this material realm.

I clutch at trees. I stand upright. I can't feel my extremities anymore. The snow charges to the ground some more. It sticks to it like glue. I advance. One step. Two steps. Three steps. I sink into the snow up to my knees.

The gusts continue. They form a compact mass and encompass everything. An all-encompassing, compact mass. The ice gets in through my holes and takes my breath away.

Not far off, there is a metal clang. If there is a hare in the trap, I will gobble it up. I will bare my canines, tear into the flesh, stick my tongue in the carcass. Let it bite, let it bleed, let it spray, let it rot. The night was hard. There is hope.

Alas, an empty piece of metal: the trap was faulty. What are these snares good for now anyway? No doubt for my head. To close around my neck. But that would be pointless, because a snare works only if it is a surprise, and I can hardly surprise myself.

Night falls, and the lethargy returns. I am going to have to surrender. The forest has won. It doesn't want me anymore, and I have had enough of myself. I need a break from me. So I think back to the day Mother decided to settle into despair. She got up in the morning and said to anyone within earshot: 'I've decided to settle into despair.' Did she take herself by surprise?

I lie down feebly, coldly, carelessly. I mustn't move. I need to get colder. This is why the dead don't move: to avoid warming themselves so they can stay dead. If they were to start moving, they might come back to life. It is death's revenge on life, which in turn follows life's revenge on death. For a long time, for millennia, someone doesn't exist. He is infinitely old as a non-being. Then, the next thing you know, he is formed and exists: he takes revenge on death. Then he dies at fifty, sixty, seventy years old, when his death takes revenge on life.

I imagine myself ready, my eyes on winter. Everything is calm: there is no more shouting. I curl up in the snow like in an eiderdown. My mouth fills with murmurs. I want to get colder. There will be a place available in life once I give up mine. And death will come fast; maybe it will be nice.

The only thing I can do until then is to play at dying. To lie on the ground and act like my breathing is slowing. The tips of my ears go numb. My eyelids flutter. I drive any awareness from my head. I do not deny my thoughts: I escape them. Denying one's thoughts would be to affirm them: I escape them. I free myself of them. I have no more evidence of myself. I have no more crass consciousness. I am just an empty form for mutating matter. I don't just cool down, I get rid of myself. I act completely naturally, as is my heredity, and I use 'I' only out of convention.

There. It's done. I am nowhere.

Rooted in nothing.

Released from everything.

Withdrawn from the past, present, and future.

Spread every which way.

And I have to accept it.

No words.

No movement.

No sudden starts.

So this is heavenly peace, redemption, salvation?

Nothing to see.

Nothing to say.

Nothing to do.

It is liberating at first, but ultimately, does anything come next?

I can't help it: I want what comes next.

That's enough death. I need to get moving again.

But as soon as I move, it hits me: I have no shelter, no food, no comfort. I am mad at myself for having left my family and then believing for a time that I was only half living, on a makeshift foundation, when I was with them. I was a bad girl. A very bad little girl.

I have two choices: go back to the village or convince the hunters to adopt me. Convince them to love me, to cherish me, to honour me, to keep me in sickness and in health, for richer or poorer, in good times and bad, until death do us part.

I leave the fangs and the claws behind. I turn my back on two whole weeks. Now and forever, I will truly live, really and truly, but as a little girl dissatisfied with the world she lives in.

And I will make do. I will stop believing that everything others do is done against me. And in return I will expect people to stop thinking that everything I do is done against them. I don't leave my body. No one leaves their bodies. Unless … ?

Tracks on the ground, the hunters. I step into them and note their size. Impressive: their size is impressive. In trying to match the stride, I am forced to do the splits. I don't walk in their footsteps. I jump in them. I get lighter in their tracks. I don't sink into the snow anymore. I stay the course. My steps follow one after the other with no more hesitation. I am going home. I am truly living, really and truly, in step with this disappointing world. I close my eyes. I mark my moment of rest and my emotions on the outside, but with no one to see me. The retreat lasts only a few seconds. When I open my eyes again, I see that everything is where it should be. In this cursed world, to which I know I should reconcile myself.

But why keep bringing up bitter memories? I know where I am, I now know where I will go. I am no longer in the middle of nowhere. I am at a particular place. That's the way it is. You think life has no meaning and then all of a sudden meaning smacks you in the face. I am searching: I have a quest. That's what happens to me. That's what happens to all of us.

Mother, who whispers to you from the inside now that your tapeworm is gone?

Mother, I am coming home. I am coming back to the village, and I will make peace with it one day, maybe.

XIX

En route, I get a sense of déjà vu. The trees start to look like sky. The rocks form arabesques on the mountains. There can be no doubt. It's Rivière-à-Pierre. I can close my eyes and hold my nose, but I still see the light that falls on Christ and smell the burning tires. Scenes and things fall into place. I have arrived, or almost.

The village is right there, behind the trees. If I keep going, I will spot the valley, I will take the path along the river, I will see the backs of houses again, the gardens, the road.

The road home has cost me. I am exhausted and beaten up. If I am to die, first things first, I will see the river again. Once more, just once more, the last time.

The sun drops behind the trees, and I head down into the valley. I will descend until I can descend no more. Before me, scraggy trees grow, hunched over. Blame the wind. On the left, there is an expanse of wild fields that give no clue as to their purpose. On the right, the earth waits to be ploughed by a farmer who can't bear the thought of unstumped land. When summer returns, the lupines will fill the ditches. But for now, it is winter.

The sun never loses faith: once it leaves Christ's face, it heads toward the cliffs, where a cross has been erected. Sometimes, the cross throws itself in the river. But for the moment, it is intact. Praise be to God.

The coast is clear. There is no one on the riverbank. All I have to do is to cross the road and I will have both feet in the sand. I close my eyes. One step. Two steps. The air, the wind, the seaweed, the waves, I open my eyes. The roaring river and the end of nothing and everything.

The boats are back in their moorings, and the villagers have forgotten about me. Slabs of ice drift in the water. My feet test it tentatively. The cold travels up through my veins, and I can hardly feel my head, barely feel my legs.

The lumberjacks are getting ready to come home. I have to take my place in the world again or a place will be forced upon me. I sense the presence of the grey house behind me. I am not yet ready to face it. Maybe Mother is sitting on the porch, wrapped in rags like a straitjacket. Maybe she is lying on the ground, holding what I used to write against her heart, near the breasts I suckled not long ago.

I walk along the riverbank, my profile to the river. So many doors could open at any moment. So many hands could grab me and lock me away. So many fingers could pull out my hair and my whiskers. I am eleven years old, and at eleven, you shouldn't be afraid anymore. Unless … ?

I remember. The caravans lined the beach. Lanterns lit the way. The music box was playing. No one was sleepy that week. People came and went from the carnival trailers at all hours of the day and night. A pleasant memory: I couldn't walk yet, and Father carried me on his shoulders. I wasn't that old, although I was no longer a fetus. I wasn't old enough to enter the cabinets of curiosities, but I remember, painted on each caravan, strange images of monstrous people, a woman with no legs, a man with no arms, a baby in a jar. I would have liked to have seen them in real life, but you had to pay.

I am on planet Earth, and it is inhabited by humans. I would like for a human to hear my confession. Are there any humans in Rivière-à-Pierre? Real humans, just humans, any human will do. I am eleven years old, and what I have to say is important. What I do has weight and has to resonate with other humans.

If I stop advancing along the beach, maybe I can spend a little longer on the inside. Here, in the village, my existence on the inside causes panic. My inside is a terrible outside in the eyes of others. And the inside of others is just as terrible in my eyes.

I left the village. Horrified, the village sent men after me. They weren't looking for me for no reason: they did it to better ostracize me, but maybe they did it to rescue me too.

I draw closer to the porches overlooking the water. They are rickety. Their wood creaks. They are bent, broken, and twisted. They have a distinct curve like old wood good for nothing but the sea. They are fragile, bent, broken, ready to tumble into the water. They are porches, and their purpose is to welcome me. I just have to step onto them by putting one foot in front of the other.

Muffled laughter reaches my ears. A light on the second floor, at the home of the widow, who is also bent and broken. You can read her windows like an open book. I clutch at the railing. I see two naked bodies through the window. A woman from behind, alive. And a man. Also alive. He leans on the woman's back. Their hands stroke each other's difference. They gnaw on each other, their skin melts together. It's like a single, teeming mass.

The man grabs the woman's hair. He bridles her. Words come out of his mouth, replacing the moans. He tells her she belongs to him. She confirms that this is so. The man's breathing speeds up, and he turns her, shoves her at his leisure. He inserts his face between two bars in front of the window. I enter his line of sight, but he doesn't see me. The woman caresses his face, a naked face from another place. He smiles tenderly, completely deforming his features. As he smiles, his beardless face morphs into one I know.

Clairmont. The word escapes my lips before I can stop it. As I say it, Clairmont almost spots me. I lose my balance and fall on a rusty nail. A bit of blood. No pus. Jealousy, fear, and pain rise into my stomach. Every step I take to get away is like three. Clairmont has lost face. He got rid of his beard and his charm along with it. He cut off his wisdom for the sake of an embrace.

I run, I escape, I don't want to alert anyone. I want to keep this quiet. No one must know that the girl who left her mother has finally come home. It is my duty to visit Mother without raising a fuss.

The road home seems long. At any moment, the local men could grab me, press me against their bodies. Make me obey. Make me grow up.

I finally see it again, the dormer window through which I watched the world. The middleman that, every night, or almost, gave me access to the river. As I approach, I see the door of the house. I notice the lock, its unique bumps, a key hidden under a board.

The house is unscathed. The door isn't open, but it certainly could be. I brave the steps, advance along the porch and make a few boards creak. Inside the walls, a thin candle is burning down. Beside it, a silhouette of someone seated, rocking. This person is waiting. She is used to waiting.

I can make out my own reflection in the half-open window. I hesitate, I step back. I have wrinkles, and there's greyish-green dried mud caked in my beard. I can't go inside without being presentable. I want to see Mother face to face, but since I ran away, will she still be able to settle for my face, with me, just me?

I find the razor in my pocket without having to search. I hesitate. The blade snakes between my fingers, then returns to my pocket. The razor is back in my hand, then back in my pocket. I take it out once and for all, and I scrape it over my face, once, twice, three times. The movement gets sharper and sharper, more and more confident. With each stroke of the blade, I grow stronger. I am dripping droplets of blood. I lose weight, I gain levity. I feel young, decidedly young.

The silhouette hasn't moved. She is still sitting and rocking. I'm finally ready to be reunited with her in this world where we both live. I slip the key into the lock and grab the doorknob. If I go in, I will show myself to her right away. If I go in, I won't be able to go out again. A gust of wind makes the shutters slam. The light hits my face. I step forward. My weight makes the porch creak.

The silhouette turns. Mother, Mother. I hesitate. I turn my head, and I see my reflection in the window pane.

Faced with my reflection, I see, with no small measure of pain and horror:

My beard grew back as I walked in the house.

Julie Demers was born in Quebec City in 1987, grew up in Drummondville, and now lives in Montreal. The French edition of this book, *Barbe*, was her first novel and was nominated for the Prix CALQ, the first-novel festival of Chambéry in France, the Grand Prix Littéraire Archambault, and was part of the Biennale littéraire des Cèdres. A film studies graduate, she heads up workshops across Canada on Quebec cinema, and her work has appeared in many culture magazines.

Rhonda Mullins has translated many books into English, including Dominique Fortier's *The Island of Books*, Elise Turcotte's *Guyana*, Louis Carmain's *Guano* and Anaïs Barbeau-Lavalette's *Suzanne*. Her translation of Jocelyne Saucier's *And the Birds Rained Down* was a contender for the 2015 Canada Reads, and she won the Governor General's Literary Award for Translation for Saucier's *Twenty-One Cardinals*.

Typeset in Oneleigh, a playful and expressive face designed by Nick Shinn in 1999. Oneleigh has obvious roots in traditional roman serifed types, however this face takes on an eccentric character of its own due to its unique forms and loose, almost hand-drawn appearance in both display and text settings, making it very lively on the page.

Printed at the Coach House on bpNichol Lane in Toronto, Ontario, on Zephyr Antique Laid paper, which was manufactured, acid-free, in Saint-Jérôme, Quebec, from second-growth forests. This book was printed with vegetable-based ink on a 1973 Heidelberg KORD offset litho press. Its pages were folded on a Baumfolder, gathered by hand, bound on a Sulby Auto-Minabinda and trimmed on a Polar single-knife cutter.

Edited and designed by Alana Wilcox
Cover design by Ingrid Paulson
Author photo of Julie Demers by Brigitte Soucy
Author photo of Rhonda Mullins by Owen Egan

Coach House Books
80 bpNichol Lane
Toronto ON M5S 3J4
Canada

416 979 2217
800 367 6360

mail@chbooks.com
www.chbooks.com